Humphrey's
Big Birthday Bash

Look for all of
HUMPHREY'S TINY TALES

Humphrey's
Big Birthday Bash

Betty G. Birney

illustrated by Priscilla Burris

G. P. PUTNAM'S SONS

G. P. PUTNAM'S SONS
an imprint of Penguin Random House LLC
375 Hudson Street
New York, NY 10014

Text copyright © 2018 by Betty G. Birney.
Illustrations copyright © 2018 by Priscilla Burris.
Penguin supports copyright. Copyright fuels creativity, encourages diverse voices, promotes
free speech, and creates a vibrant culture. Thank you for buying an authorized edition of this
book and for complying with copyright laws by not reproducing, scanning, or distributing any
part of it in any form without permission. You are supporting writers and allowing Penguin to
continue to publish books for every reader.

G. P. Putnam's Sons is a registered trademark of Penguin Random House LLC.

Library of Congress Cataloging-in-Publication Data
Names: Birney, Betty G., author. | Burris, Priscilla, illustrator.
Title: Humphrey's big birthday bash / Betty G. Birney ; illustrated by Priscilla Burris.
Description: New York, NY : G. P. Putnam's Sons, [2018]
Summary: "The students in Room 26 are throwing a birthday party, and Humphrey
is surprised when he finds out who it's for!"—Provided by publisher.
Identifiers: LCCN 2017053079 (print) | LCCN 2017061076 (ebook) | ISBN 9781524737221
(ebook) | ISBN 9781524737207 (hardcover) | ISBN 9781524737214 (paperback)
Subjects: | CYAC: Birthdays—Fiction. | Parties—Fiction. | Hamsters—Fiction. | Schools—Fiction.
Classification: LCC PZ7.B5229 (ebook) | LCC PZ7.B5229 Hn 2018 (print) | DDC [Fic]—dc23
LC record available at https://lccn.loc.gov/2017053079

Printed in the United States of America.
ISBN: 9781524737207 (hardcover)
ISBN: 9781524737214 (paperback)
1 3 5 7 9 10 8 6 4 2

Design by Eileen Savage.
Text set in ITC Stone Informal Std Medium.

To my sister-in-law, Virginia Birney,
who has always been a good friend
to Humphrey and me
—B.B.

For my Garcia and Burris family
—P.B.

Contents

BIRTHDAYS- BIRTHDAYS- BIRTHDAYS

Lots of exciting things happen in Room 26 of Longfellow School.

I see them all because I live there. I am the classroom hamster.

But I think the best part of

Gail
March 8

Art
March 16

A.J.
April 3

the day is when my friends come bursting through the door in the morning. They always have cheerful hellos, and they tell me about their news.

One morning, Kirk came into our classroom and said, "Happy birthday to me!"

Mandy looked puzzled. She stared at the row of cupcakes above the chalkboard and frowned.

2

Sometimes when I look at those cupcakes, my tail twitches and my whiskers wiggle. They look so YUMMY-YUMMY-YUMMY!

The problem is, they're not real cupcakes. They're just pictures of cupcakes with candles on top. Each one has a name and a date.

The cupcakes help us remember when a classmate has a birthday.

One thing I've learned from

humans—birthdays are very important!

"It's *not* your birthday, Kirk," Mandy said.

Mandy Payne is a nice girl, but she does like to complain. I

call her Don't-Complain-Mandy-Payne.

"It's *almost* my birthday," Kirk said. "It will be on Friday."

Mandy started shaking her head. "No, it won't!" she insisted loudly.

Our teacher, Mrs. Brisbane, asked, "What's the problem?"

"Kirk says it's his birthday on Friday, but it's not." Mandy pointed to the cupcakes. "See? His birthday is on Saturday."

Mrs. Brisbane nodded. "Yes.

But since we don't have school on Saturday, we're celebrating Kirk's birthday on Friday."

"Fine," Mandy said. "But he shouldn't say it's his birthday when it's not."

"Please Don't-Complain-Mandy-Payne," Mrs. Brisbane said.

"Hey, Mandy, I've got a joke for you," Kirk said.

He *loves* to tell jokes, and I think he wanted to make Mandy smile.

"What do you give a nine-hundred-pound gorilla for his birthday?" he asked.

"I don't know," Mandy answered.

"Anything he wants!" Kirk said, howling with laughter.

Some of my other friends laughed, too, like Stop-Giggling-Gail. She is almost always laughing.

"Anything he wants!" Repeat-It-Please-Richie said.

Richie, A.J. and Garth beat their chests and made grunting

sounds. I think they were pre-tending to be gorillas.

Just then, the bell rang. School was starting, so my friends all sat down.

After Mrs. Brisbane took attendance, Kirk raised his hand.

"Mrs. Brisbane, am I going to be able to take Humphrey home for the weekend, like you said?" he asked.

I live in Room 26, but I'm LUCKY-LUCKY-LUCKY that I get to go home with my friends on weekends.

Our teacher nodded. "Yes, Kirk."

"Good," Kirk said. "He'll be there for my birthday *hsab*. Everyone in class is invited."

Hsab? What was that strange word?

The way he said it sounded like "huh-sab."

Mrs. Brisbane gave him a funny look. "I'm glad everyone is invited," she said. "But I've never heard of a *hsab* before. What does it mean?"

"I can't tell you!" Kirk grinned broadly. "H-S-A-B. You have to

work it out for yourselves. That's part of the fun."

"Maybe if we look at the word, it will help," Mrs. Brisbane said. She wrote the strange word on the board in big letters: *HSAB*.

We all looked at it for a few seconds, but I don't think it helped.

Then Mrs. Brisbane began teaching the class about numbers.

She said something about Jonny having twelve apples and Suzy taking away eight. I don't know Suzy, but I hope she asked Jonny before she took away his apples!

I tried to pay attention to what Mrs. Brisbane was saying, but my mind kept wandering to the word on the board.

Hsab. What on earth could it mean?

Later that night, I turned to my neighbor, Og the Frog. He is the other classroom pet. His tank sits next to my cage.

"Do you know what *hsab* means?" I asked.

"BOING!" he replied.

He makes a funny sound, but he's really very nice for a frog.

"Me neither," I said.

I took out the little notebook and pencil that I keep hidden behind the mirror in my cage. I wrote down the word so I could take a closer look.

H S A B

I turned the page sideways. I turned it so the word was upside down. It still didn't make sense. Then I flipped the notebook over so I couldn't see the word anymore.

But I could see the mirror. In the mirror, everything looks backwards, including words.

This word looked STRANGE-STRANGE-STRANGE.

I saw a backwards *B*, an *A*, a backwards *S* and an *H*. In that order, the word would be *B-A-S-H*.

A *bash*! A bash is a great, big, wonderful party.

So Kirk was having a birthday bash!

But why did he write the word backwards? Humans are nice, but sometimes they do very strange things.

~~~

I wasn't the only one in Room 26 who had worked out that *hsab* was *bash* spelled backwards.

As Lower-Your-Voice-A.J. came into class the next morning, he shouted, "It's a birthday bash! I got the invitation, and my mom held it up to the mirror. Some of the letters were backwards, but she worked it out."

A.J.'s mom must be SMART-SMART-SMART (like me).

Mrs. Brisbane asked Kirk to explain why he had written the words that way.

"It's a backwards party," he said. "Everything will be backwards. Hands down if you're coming."

Some of my friends raised up their hands.

"*Down,*" Kirk said. "Everything is backwards."

There were some giggles and then every one of them waved a hand down at the floor. My paw went down, too.

"It sounds like a very interesting party," Mrs. Brisbane said.

"Mrs. Brisbane?" Mandy said. "I've been looking at the birthday cupcakes, and some names are missing."

Our teacher looked up at the row of cupcakes.

"Yours isn't there," Mandy continued. "Or Humphrey's."

I scrambled to the tippy top of my cage to see if she was right. Sure enough, Mrs. Brisbane's name wasn't there, and neither was mine.

18

Another name was also missing.

"What about Og?" I squeaked at the top of my tiny lungs.

"Oooh, Og's birthday is missing, too," Raise-Your-Hand-Heidi said. As usual, she forgot to raise her hand.

I was glad that Heidi had also noticed that Og's name was missing. When I squeak, humans can't understand me.

"I don't need everyone to remember my birthday," Mrs. Brisbane said. "Every day I'm

here in Room Twenty-six is a special day for me."

My friends still wanted to know about Og and me.

"The problem is, I don't know when they were born," Mrs. Brisbane said.

I suddenly felt SAD-SAD-SAD. If no one knew when I was born, I could never have a birthday!

Heidi said, "Frogs aren't born. They're hatched!"

"That's right," Mrs. Brisbane said. "Frogs start out as eggs."

Og splashed around a little in his tank.

I felt SAD-SAD-SAD for him, too. He could never have a birthday. He could have a hatchday, but nobody knew when it was.

A SILLY-SILLY-SILLY Party

On Friday, we celebrated Kirk's birthday in class.

First, he got to wear a shiny birthday crown all day.

Next, he got to pick a gift from

Mrs. Brisbane's birthday grab bag.

She asked him to close his eyes and reach inside. He pulled out a big sheet of silly stickers.

I was glad it was something funny, since Kirk likes to joke around.

Then we all sang him a birthday song. I happily squeaked along, and I even heard a few BOING-BOINGs coming from Og.

At the end of the day, Kirk's mom came to pick us up.

"Bye, Og," I squeaked. "I'll tell you all about the bash on Monday."

Og doesn't leave Room 26 on the weekends because he can go a few days without being fed.

I didn't like leaving him behind. He didn't have his own hatchday, *and* he wasn't going to Kirk's birthday hsab.

I guess it's not easy being a frog.

~~~~~

The next day, it was time for the party. Kirk set me on a big table near the front door. I could see everything.

"Just watch, Humphrey," he said. "The fun is about to begin."

Something funny had already begun, because Kirk had his shirt on backwards. There was a pocket on his back!

Most of his clothes were on backwards, except his shoes. I think it would be hard for a human to walk in backwards shoes. It would be hard for a hamster to walk in shoes at all!

The doorbell rang and Kirk ran to open it. "Good-bye," he said to Richie.

When Richie tried to take a step into the house, Kirk said,

"Not like that!" Kirk turned Richie around and said, "You have to come in backwards."

So Richie came through the door walking backwards.

And that wasn't the only strange thing. He was also wearing his clothes inside out!

All my friends from Room 26 arrived wearing their clothes

backwards or inside out. They all
loved the birthday balloons, which
were sitting on the floor instead
of floating near the ceiling.

And they laughed at the music. It sounded STRANGE-STRANGE-STRANGE because it was playing backwards.

Then Kirk moved my cage to the backyard, where my friends had a relay race.

It was so funny to see them running backwards. They flapped their arms and bumped into each other, laughing all the time.

I laughed, too.

At last, it was time to eat.

All my friends ran inside and gathered around a big table. Kirk put my cage on a little one right next to it.

Kirk's mom brought out the birthday cake. On top, there was writing in bright red icing.

I had a pretty good idea that those letters spelled out HAPPY BIRTHDAY, KIRK—only backwards!

Singing the birthday song backwards wasn't easy. Kirk's dad had printed out the words so everyone could read them, but it was still hard.

Then, instead of blowing out his birthday candles, Kirk helped his mom light them.

"Make a wish," Kirk's mom said.

Kirk closed his eyes and opened

them again. Then he blew out the candles.

But the strange thing was, they lit right up again!

Kirk tried to blow them out again and again, but the flames kept coming back. They were trick candles!

"Backwards candles," Kirk said. "Awesome!"

Finally, Kirk's dad put them out. He cut pieces of cake for everyone. Then, Kirk's mom scooped ice cream.

"Hey, what did the ice cream say to the cake?" Kirk asked.

No one answered, so Kirk said, "'What's eating you?'"

I laughed and laughed—it was such a funny joke!

~~~~~

Kirk's friends gave him presents wrapped with inside-out paper. Some had bows tied on the bottom instead of the top.

He got a toy helicopter, some

rocks for his rock collection, a board game and a joke book.

I think the joke book was his favorite present, because he started reading it right away.

"Hey, what does a cat eat for his birthday?" he asked. "*Mice* cream and cake!"

Everybody laughed except me. After all, mice and hamsters are a lot alike.

I was SO-SO-SO embarrassed because I didn't have a present for Kirk.

Then I had an idea. I might

not have had a present, but at least I could add something to the party.

I decided to put on a show.

First, I started spinning on my wheel.

Richie heard it squeak. "Hey, look at Humphrey go!" he said.

Soon, all my friends were gathered around my cage, watching.

I hopped off my wheel and climbed up the big tree branch in my cage, all the way to the top.

"Oooh," my friends said.

Then I grabbed onto the top bars and made a daring jump straight down, landing in my soft bedding.

"Aaah!" everyone said.

To finish off the act, I got back on the wheel—but this time, I ran backwards as fast as I could.

It wasn't easy, but it was worth it because my friends all clapped for me.

When it was time for the guests to leave, everyone said "hello," which made me giggle.

"Hello!" I squeaked loudly.

After everyone had gone home, Kirk said, "Thank you, Humphrey, for helping make my party turn out so well!"

"Thanks for inviting me," I squeaked back.

I don't think I'd ever had so

much fun in my life. I only wished
Og could have been there, too.

~~~~~

When I got back to Room 26 on
Monday morning, I was starting
to tell my froggy friend about the
backwards bash. But I heard Garth
say, "Listen up, everybody."

He looked over at my cage.
Then he glanced at the door,
where Mrs. Brisbane was talking
to the teacher across the hall.

"I have a great idea. Want to hear it?" Garth asked in a loud whisper.

"Yes!" the other students answered.

"YES-YES-YES!" I squeaked.

"Quiet, everyone," he said. "It's a secret." Garth turned to Richie and whispered something in his ear.

All I could hear were the words *surprise* and *Friday*.

I like surprises and wanted to hear more. "Could you squeak up just a little?" I asked.

Richie turned to Miranda and whispered in her ear.

I perked up my tiny pink ears, but all I could hear was the word *present*.

Miranda smiled. "Oooh, I have an idea!"

"*Shhh*," the other children told her.

"Sorry," Miranda said softly. Then she turned to Gail and whispered in her ear.

Gail giggled, then whispered in A.J.'s ear.

This time, I heard the word *birthday*.

Next, A.J. whispered in Kirk's ear. Even when he whispers, A.J. is loud. But I couldn't hear everything he said. I only heard him say *Mrs. Brisbane*.

Surprise. Friday. Present. Birthday. Mrs. Brisbane.

So *that* was the secret! They were having a surprise birthday party for Mrs. Brisbane on Friday!

My whiskers wiggled at the exciting news. But I wished my friends had whispered in my ear, too, so I'd know more about the plans.

Mrs. Brisbane came over to the group. "Why are you all whispering?" she asked.

"It's a secret," A.J. said.

Mrs. Brisbane smiled. "As long as it's a good secret, I guess that's okay." She glanced over at my cage and said, "Isn't that right, Humphrey?"

I wasn't sure if secrets were ever okay. But this was a good one for sure.

Before I could answer, the bell rang and Mrs. Brisbane started class.

I always try to listen to every word she says. But it wasn't easy. My mind was racing with thoughts about her surprise birthday party.

Would it be backwards or forward?

Would there be games?

And most important, would there be yummy cake?

The GREAT-
GREAT-GREAT
Escape

The next few days, I was HAPPY-HAPPY-HAPPY all the time.

I thought about how happy Mrs. Brisbane would be on Friday

when the whole class shouted, "Surprise!"

When my friends whispered about presents, I thought about how she'd smile when she opened her gifts.

I even practiced the birthday song in my mirror. This time, I squeaked it forward, not backwards.

But I was puzzled by a few things that happened during the week.

On Tuesday, Sayeh and Seth

suddenly started measuring my cage with a ruler. They also measured Og's tank.

"It's for a math problem," Sayeh told us.

Sometimes Mrs. Brisbane has students measure things for math, so I guess that made sense.

On Wednesday, Mandy raised her hand and asked how to spell my name.

Mrs. Brisbane wrote *Humphrey* on the board. She also let the students work a lot longer than usual on their art. And some of them worked with their backs toward me so I couldn't see what they were doing. They'd never done that before.

On Thursday night, I made myself get some sleep. Even though hamsters like me are often awake at night, I didn't want to be tired during Mrs. Brisbane's surprise party the next day.

I dozed for a while, and I had very strange dreams.

First, I dreamed about YUMMY-YUMMY-YUMMY dancing cupcakes.

Then I dreamed about the look on Mrs. Brisbane's face when she saw her gifts and cake and we all squeaked "Happy Birthday" to her.

Suddenly, I woke up with a terrible thought.

"Og!" I squeaked. "We forgot something."

Og splashed around in his tank.

I jiggled the lock on my cage door. It seems tightly locked, but I have a secret way to open it. That's why I call it the lock-that-doesn't-lock.

I jiggled the lock some more and the door opened. I hurried across the table to Og's tank.

"Og, we forgot to get a present for Mrs. Brisbane!" I told him.

"Just like I forgot to get one for Kirk!"

"BOING-BOING!" he answered loudly.

"We have to give her something so she'll know we're glad she's our teacher," I explained. "But what?"

Og stared at me from his tank, but he didn't answer.

I guess it was up to me to think of an idea.

We couldn't buy something from a store, so we'd have to make her a gift.

I looked up at the chalkboard, with the row of cupcakes above it.

"I know," I said. "Let's make her a cake. After all, you can't have too much cake at a birthday party!"

"BOING-BOING-BOING!" Og hopped up and down.

"Of course, we can't *bake* a cake," I said. "But we can make her a hamster-and-frog kind of cake."

"BOING!" Og agreed.

I went back into my cage. I was delighted to see that my food dish was full of crunchy Nutri-Nibbles. They are yummy-yummy-yummy!

They aren't soft enough to make into a cake, but I had an idea.

One by one, I put a few Nutri-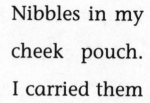Nibbles in my cheek pouch. I carried them out of the cage and set them down in front of Og's tank. After a while, I had a nice stack of them.

"I need your help, Og," I said.

"BOING-BOING!" he answered.

"Splash a lot of water so it goes on the Nutri-Nibbles," I said. Then I scampered out of the way because water isn't good for hamsters.

Og's tank has a lid, but it's full of holes. So if he splashes hard enough, some of the water can fly out of the top.

He splashed . . . and splashed some more.

Soon, the pile of Nutri-Nibbles was nice and wet.

"Thanks, Og," I said.

Then I went straight to work. With my paws, I patted and smoothed the Nutri-Nibbles into a circle.

"It *looks* like a cake," I said. "But it's awfully plain."

"BOING-BOING," Og agreed.

So I went back into my cage and dug around in my bedding. Sometimes I store food there.

I found two dried strawberries and three raisins and pressed them into the top of the cake.

Next, I scurried to the back of

the table, where Mrs. Brisbane keeps food and supplies for Og and me.

There were big bags of Mighty Mealworms, Healthy Dots, Nutri-Nibbles, Hamster Chew-Chews and nice, soft hay. Yum!

I also found a box of Og's Froggy Fish Sticks and a can of crickets!

(Yep, that's what frogs eat. Eww!)

The Froggy Fish Sticks didn't look like anything I'd want to eat, but they did look a lot like birthday candles. I held my breath and stuck my head into the box.

I grabbed a Froggy Fish Stick and quickly came up for air. They smelled even worse than I'd imagined.

Then I scrambled back to the top of the cake. I stuck the stinky stick right in the middle.

"BOING-BOING-BOING!" Og called out. "BOING-BOING-BOING-*BOING*!"

I thought the cake looked great, but Og seemed a little *too* excited about it.

"Just one more thing," I told him. "I think a few Healthy Dots would look nice."

Healthy Dots are good for hamsters. Also, they are many different colors and look like candy.

Og splashed crazily in his tank, but I scurried to the back of the table once again.

I was trying to work out how to close the box when I heard people talking.

Then Og started twanging. "BOING-BOING-*BOING!*"

I couldn't see anything, but when I heard A.J.'s loud voice, I knew my friends had come into the classroom.

I looked up at the window. It was already light outside!

Then I heard Mrs. Brisbane say, "Good morning." And the bell rang.

The school day was starting and I was nowhere near my cage!

I was STUCK-STUCK-STUCK.

A BIG-BIG-BIG
Surprise

Mrs. Brisbane took attendance.

I heard Heidi say, "Can we do it now?" It was an odd thing to say, but she sounded very excited.

"I think we should wait until

just before recess," Mrs. Brisbane said.

They kept talking, but I couldn't hear well from my hiding place. If only I could see what was going on!

I thought I heard Garth ask, "Where's Humphrey? I don't see him."

Then Mrs. Brisbane said something about me making a map. Or maybe she said I was taking a nap.

I would have been so happy to be taking a nap instead of being stuck outside my cage.

I wasn't exactly sure what would happen next. Maybe my friends would learn I was missing and find out about the lock-that-doesn't-lock.

If they fixed it, I'd be trapped in my cage forever!

Or maybe no one would notice I wasn't in my cage. Then I'd miss out on Mrs. Brisbane's birthday party!

I didn't like either of those ideas one bit.

Og splashed nervously in his tank.

I crossed my toes and hoped that everyone would leave the classroom so I could return to my cage. Or maybe my friends would get so busy that I could sneak back without them noticing.

But I heard Mrs. Brisbane say, "It's time."

That was odd, too, because the birthday party was supposed to be a surprise for *her*.

Next, I heard lots of whispering and rustling. Footsteps came closer and closer.

I heard Gail giggle, and someone said, "Shhh!"

Then Mrs. Brisbane whispered, "Ready?"

Suddenly, all of my classmates screamed, "SURPRISE!"

"Come on out, Humphrey Dumpty," A.J. shouted. "It's time for your birthday party!"

Sayeh's softer voice said, "And Og's hatchday party."

"BOING!" Og said.

My birthday party? Og's hatchday party?

I was amazed. The surprise party wasn't for Mrs. Brisbane. It was for Og and me.

But the biggest surprise was the fact that I was missing my own celebration!

"Where is he?" Richie asked.

Og splashed wildly. I think he was as confused as I was.

"Come on out, Humphrey. We want to wish you a happy birthday," Mrs. Brisbane said.

I didn't know what to do, so I sat and waited.

Mrs. Brisbane told someone to open the cage. A few seconds later, I heard Garth say, "He's not here!"

Of course, everyone thought that was impossible.

There were more rustling noises.

"You're right," Mrs. Brisbane said. "I don't think Humphrey's in his cage. I wonder if someone left the door unlocked. Or maybe it's broken."

I heard the cage door open
and shut a few times.

"No, Mrs. Brisbane," Art said.
"It works just fine."

"We must all look for him," Mrs. Brisbane said. "But we'll have to be very careful not to step on him."

"Eeek!" I squeaked. I didn't mean to say it, but just thinking of someone stepping on me, it came out.

"I can hear him!" Miranda said.

Oops!

There was no hiding now, so I decided it was time to show myself.

"Surprise!" I squeaked as I
scurried across the table.

"There's Humphrey Dumpty!"
A.J. shouted.

Mrs. Brisbane scooped me up
and put me back in my cage.
"Humphrey, when your friends

told me they wanted to give you a surprise party, I never dreamed you wouldn't show up for it," she said.

So, Mrs. Brisbane was in on it all along!

"I don't know how you got out,

but please don't do it again," she said to me.

I didn't squeak back to her because I was pretty sure I *would* get out of my cage again. Only next time, I wouldn't get caught.

After that, I had a wonderful time!

Sayeh put a paper birthday crown on top of my cage. Richie put one on top of Og's tank. Then they put a big banner across my cage that said, "Happy Birthday, Humphrey!"

So *that's* why they measured my cage.

Another banner went across Og's tank. It said, "Happy Hatchday, Og!"

They gave us cards they had made. And they gave us presents.

Og got a special rock that he could climb over or hide under.

And I got an amazing gift—a tiny bell that makes a nice tinkling sound when I touch it.

It was the BEST-BEST-BEST present I could imagine!

But my ears perked up when I

heard A.J.'s loud voice say, "Cake time!"

"It looks as if Humphrey already has one," Mrs. Brisbane said, leaning down to look at the tiny cake I had made. "Who made this cute little cake?" she asked.

No one answered, so I decided to squeak up. "I did," I said. "I made it for you."

Mrs. Brisbane laughed. "I guess it's a secret. But Humphrey seems to know who it was."

I DID-DID-DID!

Then I was presented with the most beautiful cake I'd ever seen. It was made of nuts and seeds and raisins—all my favorite foods!

The whole class sang the happy birthday song to me.

Next, they gave Og a cake made of smelly things he likes. They sang a happy hatchday song to him.

He splashed all around his tank.

~~~

At the end of the day, all my classmates left. Mrs. Brisbane came over to our table.

"I hope you liked your party," she said.

"It was hamster-iffic," I answered. "But it was supposed to be for *you*!"

I know that all she heard was "SQUEAK-SQUEAK-SQUEAK."

But Mrs. Brisbane laughed and said, "Happy birthday, Humphrey and Og."

I said, "Happy birthday, Mrs. Brisbane."

Og said, "BOING-BOING-BOING!"

We both agreed it really was the best birthday bash ever.

I was surprised that the party was for us and not Mrs. Brisbane. And my *friends* were surprised that I wasn't around for my own party.

"I hope we have another birthday and hatchday party next year," I told Og when we were alone for the night.

"And I still hope we have a surprise birthday party for Mrs. Brisbane," I added.

"BOING-BOING!" he said.

And then I rang my shiny new
bell a few times, just for fun.